To

....

From

....

Date

....

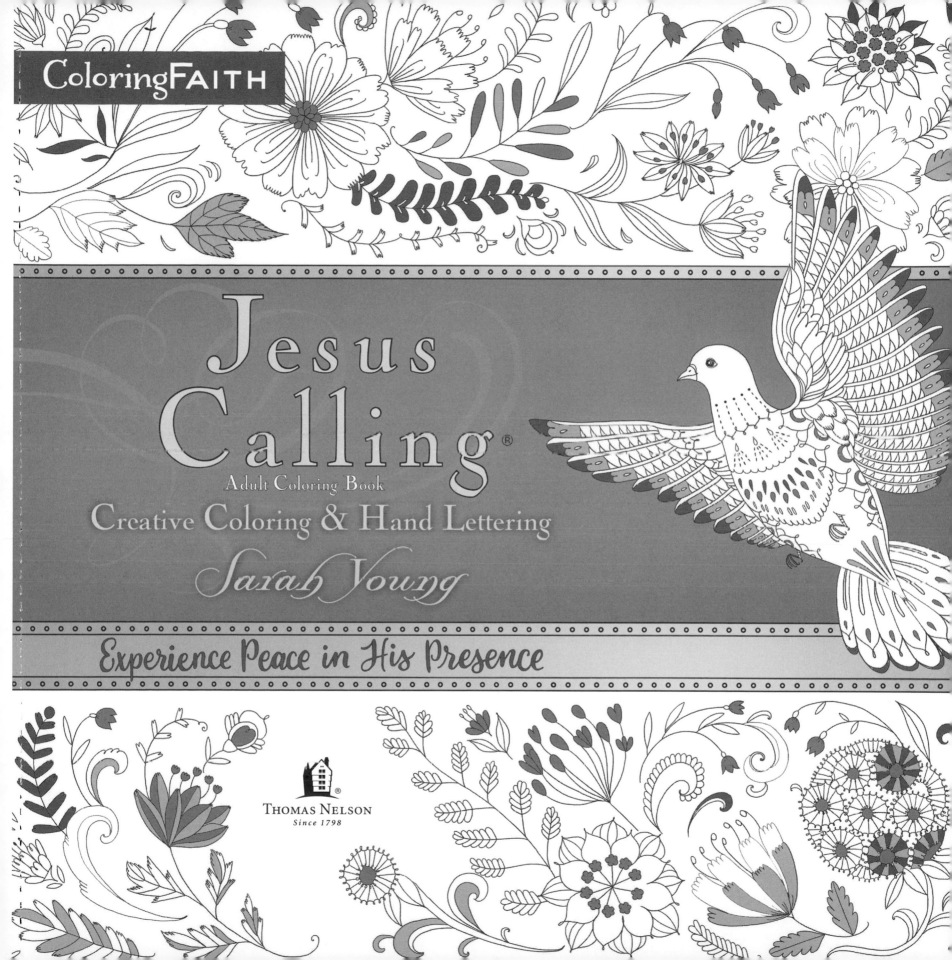

ColoringFAITH

Jesus Calling®

Adult Coloring Book

Creative Coloring & Hand Lettering

Sarah Young

Experience Peace in His Presence

THOMAS NELSON
Since 1798

Jesus Calling® *Creative Coloring and Hand Lettering Book*

Copyright © 2017 by Sarah Young

All quotes from *Jesus Calling*®.

Published in Nashville, Tennessee, by Thomas Nelson. Thomas Nelson is a registered trademark of HarperCollins Christian Publishing, Inc.

Unless otherwise noted, Scripture quotations are taken from the Holy Bible, New International Version®, NIV®. Copyright © 1973, 1978, 1984 by Biblica, Inc.® Used by permission of Zondervan. All rights reserved worldwide. www.zondervan.com. The "NIV" and "New International Version" are trademarks registered in the United States Patent and Trademark Office by Biblica, Inc.®

Other Scripture quotations are from the following sources: New King James Version®. © 1982 by Thomas Nelson. Used by permission. All rights reserved.

ISBN 978-0-7180-9126-2

Printed in China

20 21 22 23 24 /DSC/ 22 21 20 19 18 17 16 15 14

Introduction

Hand lettering is for everyone!

Hand lettering is one of the biggest trends out there. What's so fun about art—even hand lettering—is that the sky is the limit. Whether you've had formal training or just want to try your hand and have fun with it, hand lettering is for any skill level. With a few basic principles, time, and practice, you can develop your own unique style and try new and creative techniques each day.

There are so many types of lettering tools on the market that it can be a bit overwhelming. A small investment in a few tools will take you far! You can create gorgeous hand-lettered pieces with pencils, fine felt-tip markers, brush pens, watercolor brushes, and more.

In this book, in addition to gorgeous, intricate illustrations to color, you will find hand-lettering designs of quotes taken from the Bible and from Sarah Young's 365-day devotional *Jesus Calling*®. You can trace these designs with an ultra-fine marker or color them in with a paintbrush or brush pen. You'll also see that some of the words are shaded gray, which will help guide you through each stroke.

As you begin this creative journey, remember that it doesn't have to be complicated. Enjoy the practice of hand lettering as you reflect on Scripture and trace quotes that remind you of God's unending love for you. For additional help, there are lined practice pages with sample letters in the back of the book. Grab a pencil and a sheet of paper or a practice sketch pad. Trace over the sample letters or copy them side by side on your paper. You can thicken downstrokes (the lines that occur anytime you draw downward when you create letters) or you can color in downstrokes (or weight your downstrokes heavily with a brush or brush pen). Include details and swirls among the words and letters for added artistry.

Basic Principles

A few basic principles will guide your hand lettering throughout this book:

- Sketch out your ideas
- Trace and fill in
- Add details
- Mix and match fonts
- Have fun!

About This Book

This one-of-a-kind adult coloring and hand-lettering book contains more than 100 illustrations to color and hand-lettering quotes to trace. This book offers you a time to relax and think about God's Word while you create beautiful pieces of art. Quotes from the #1 bestseller *Jesus Calling*® fill these pages with themes of thankfulness and trust in the Lord and the Peace only Jesus can bring. These themes are quite prevalent in the Bible and are a vital part of a close relationship with the Lord. Experience a deeper relationship with Jesus as you focus on His words of hope, guidance, and peace.

I am far more

REAL than

the world you can

see, hear,

and touch.

Go gently through this day leaning on Me and enjoying My presence.

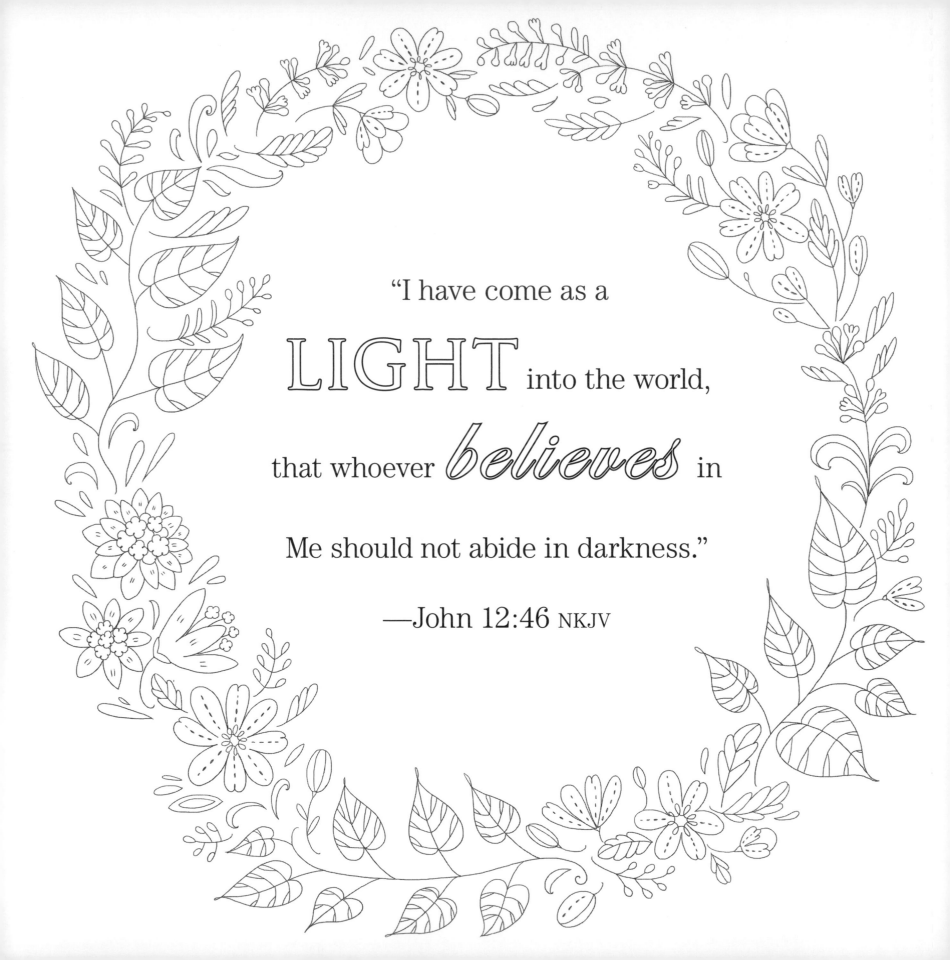

"I have come as a

LIGHT into the world,

that whoever *believes* in

Me should not abide in darkness."

—John 12:46 NKJV

I CARE AS MUCH
ABOUT YOUR

tiny
trust
'STEPS'

THROUGH DAILY LIFE
AS ABOUT YOUR
DRAMATIC

leaps
OF
faith

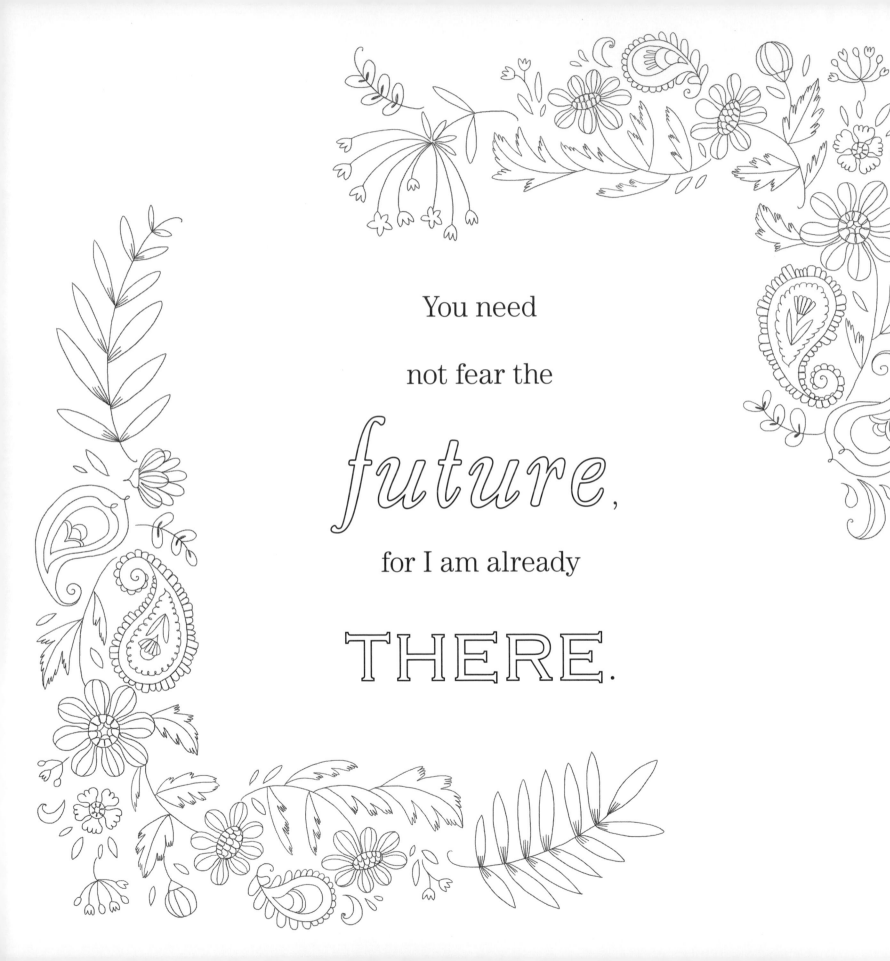

You need

not fear the

future,

for I am already

THERE.

We have this hope as an ANCHOR for the soul, firm & secure.

Hebrews 6:19

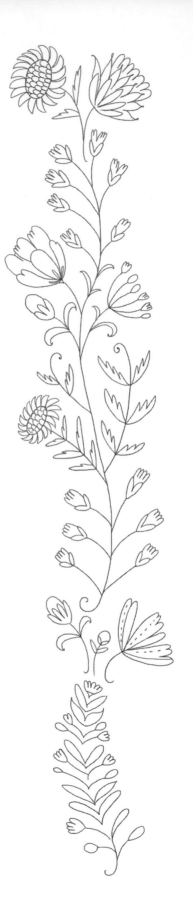

Trust and *thankfulness* will get you safely through this day. Trust PROTECTS you from worrying and obsessing. Thankfulness KEEPS you from criticizing and complaining.

I am WITH YOU & for you. YOU FACE nothing alone—NOTHING!

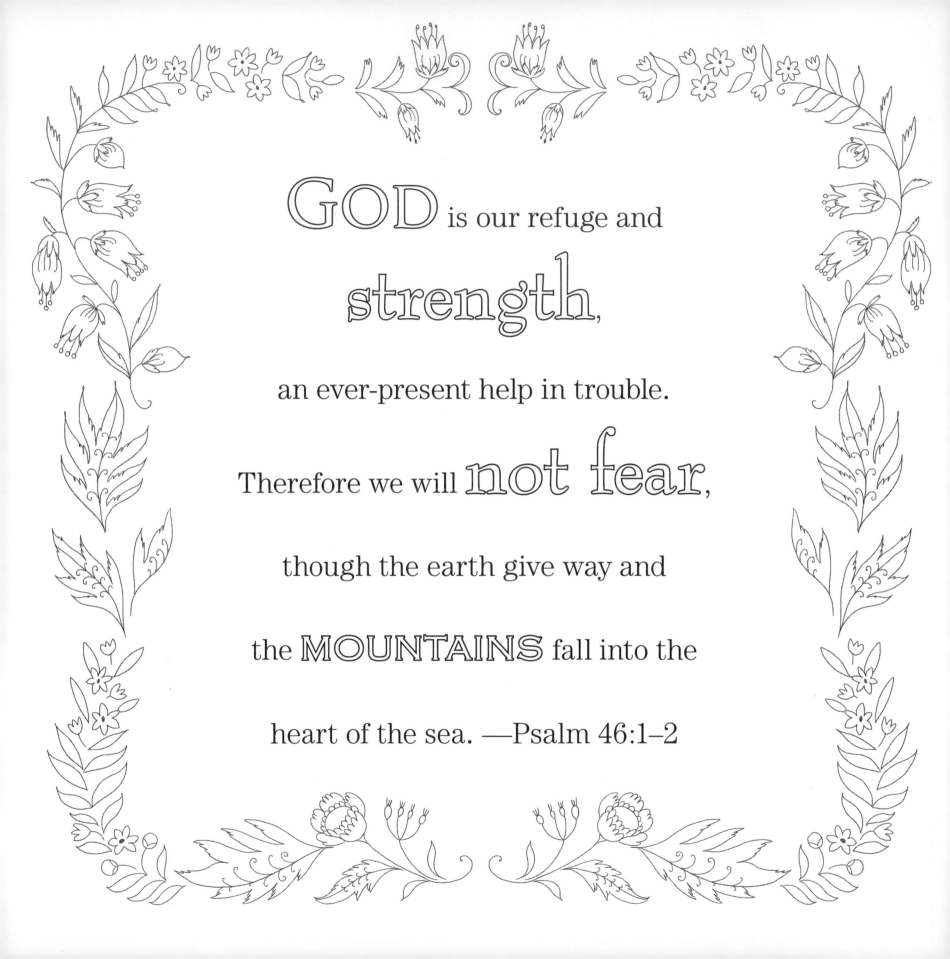

GOD is our refuge and
strength,
an ever-present help in trouble.

Therefore we will not fear,

though the earth give way and

the MOUNTAINS fall into the

heart of the sea. —Psalm 46:1–2

whenever you find yourself worrying about the future repent and return to ME.

I am *training* you to hold in your heart a dual focus: My continual Presence and the hope of HEAVEN.

TRUST is a Golden PATHWAY to HEAVEN.

WHEN YOU WALK on this path, YOU live above YOUR circumstances.

Entrust your loved ones

to Me; release them into

My protective care.

They are much safer with Me than

in your clinging hands.

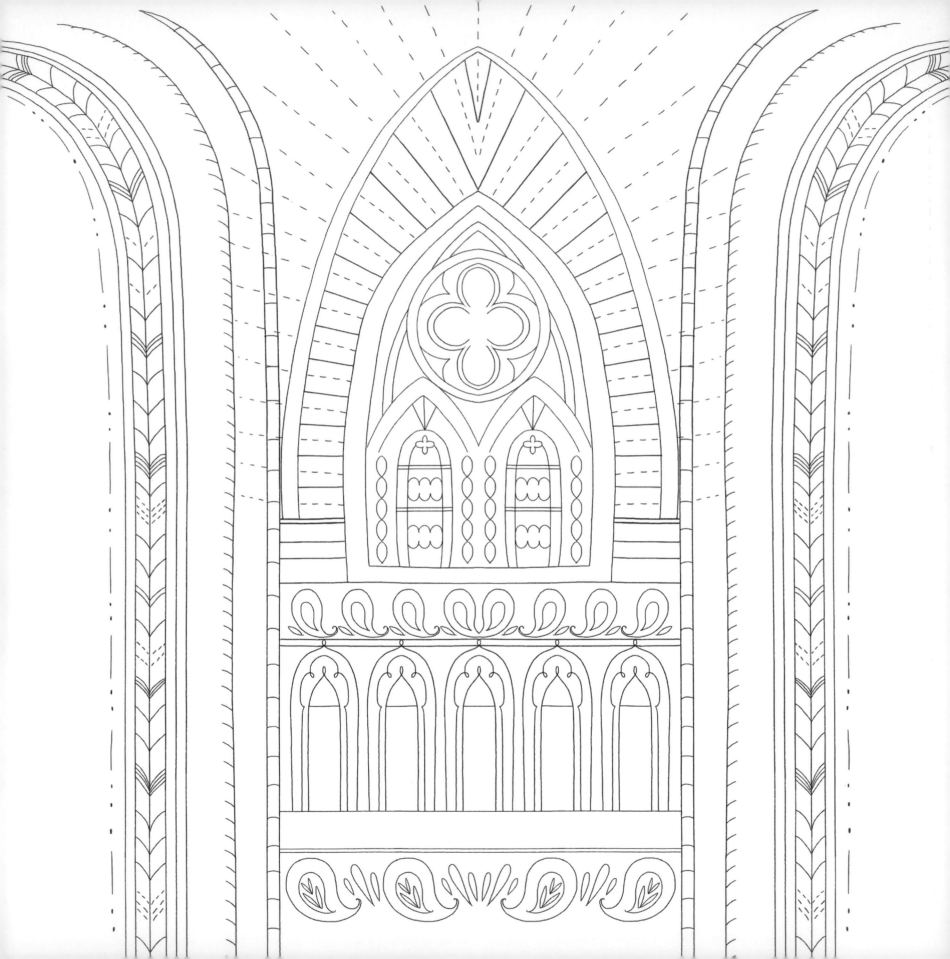

Look to the Lord and his strength, seek his face always.

1 Chronicles 16:11

My *peace* is such an all-encompassing *gift* that it is independent of all circumstances.

Though you lose everything else, if you GAIN My Peace you are *rich* indeed.

I, the Lover of your Soul, understand you perfectly AND LOVE·YOU ETERNALLY.

The way to WALK

through demanding days

is to GRIP My hand

tightly and stay in close

communication with Me.

MY kingdom IS NOT ABOUT EARNING AND DESERVING; IT IS ABOUT believing AND receiving

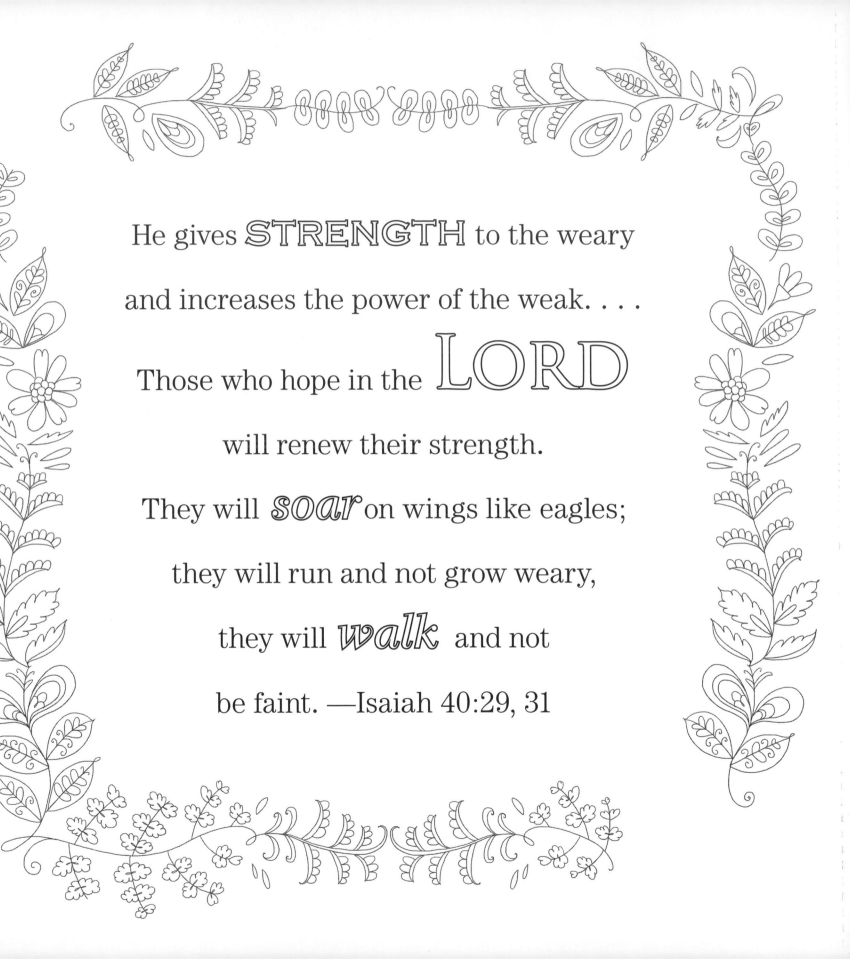

He gives STRENGTH to the weary
and increases the power of the weak. . . .
Those who hope in the LORD
will renew their strength.
They will *soar* on wings like eagles;
they will run and not grow weary,
they will *walk* and not
be faint. —Isaiah 40:29, 31

I am so nearer than you dare believe closer than the air you breathe.

I know

every

step of the

journey

ahead of you,

all the way to

heaven.

EACH MOMENT
YOU CAN CHOOSE
TO PRACTICE

My Presence

ORTO PRACTICE THE

PRESENCE OF PROBLEMS

I

COMPREHEND

you in all your complexity;

no *detail* of your

life is hidden from Me.

I VIEW you

through eyes of

grace.

I will praise you, o Lord my God, with all my heart.

Psalm 86:12 NKJV

TRUST Me in the

midst of a messy day.

Your inner CALM—

your *peace* in

My Presence—

need not be shaken by what

is going on around you.

HOPE is a golden cord connecting you to HEAVEN.

Bring me

the sacrifice of

thanksgiving.

Take nothing for granted,

not even the

rising

of the SUN.

NOTHING YOU DO OR DON'T DO CAN SEPARATE YOU FROM MY love.

Bearing your circumstances bravely—even thanking Me for them—is one of the highest forms of praise. This sacrifice of *thanksgiving* rings golden-toned bells of Joy throughout HEAVENLY realms.

You are my lamp, O Lord,
the Lord turns my darkness into light.

2 Samuel 22:29

Pray about

EVERYTHING;

then, leave

OUTCOMES

up to Me.

Receive My Peace AS YOU LIE DOWN TO Sleep, WITH thankful thoughts PLAYING A lullaby IN YOUR mind.

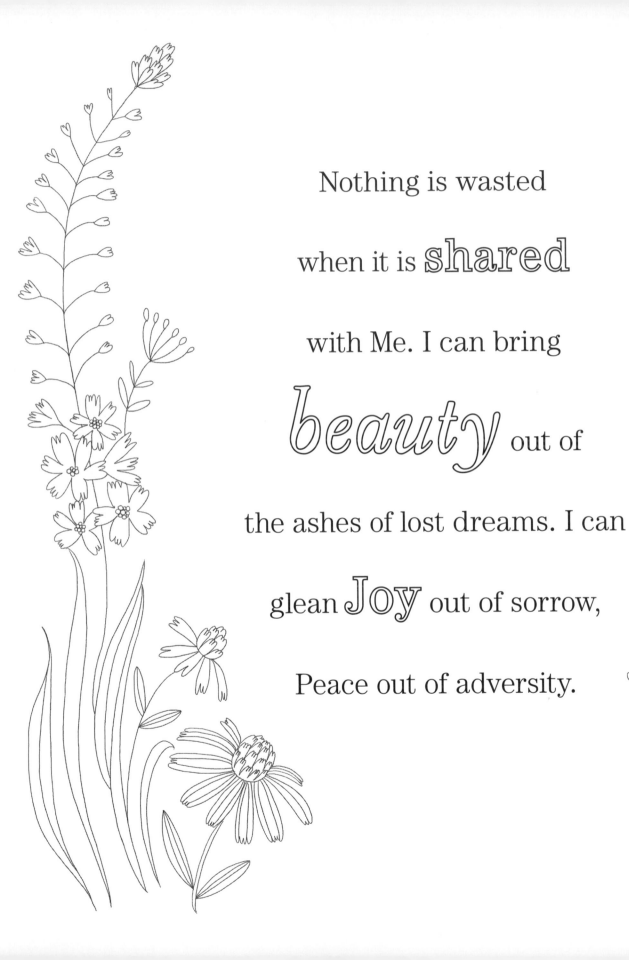

Nothing is wasted

when it is shared

with Me. I can bring

beauty out of

the ashes of lost dreams. I can

glean Joy out of sorrow,

Peace out of adversity.

Come to Me. Come to Me. Come to Me.

This is My continual invitation to you, proclaimed in

holy whispers.

Gently bring your

ATTENTION

back to Me, whenever

it wanders away. I look

for persistence—

rather than perfection—

in your WALK with Me.

O God, you are my God, earnestly I seek you.

Psalm 63:1

Every time you thank Me,

you acknowledge that I am

your LORD and PROVIDER.

This is the proper stance for a child of

God: receiving with thanksgiving.

Take a DEEP breath AND DIVE INTO THE depths OF ABSOLUTE TRUST IN ME.

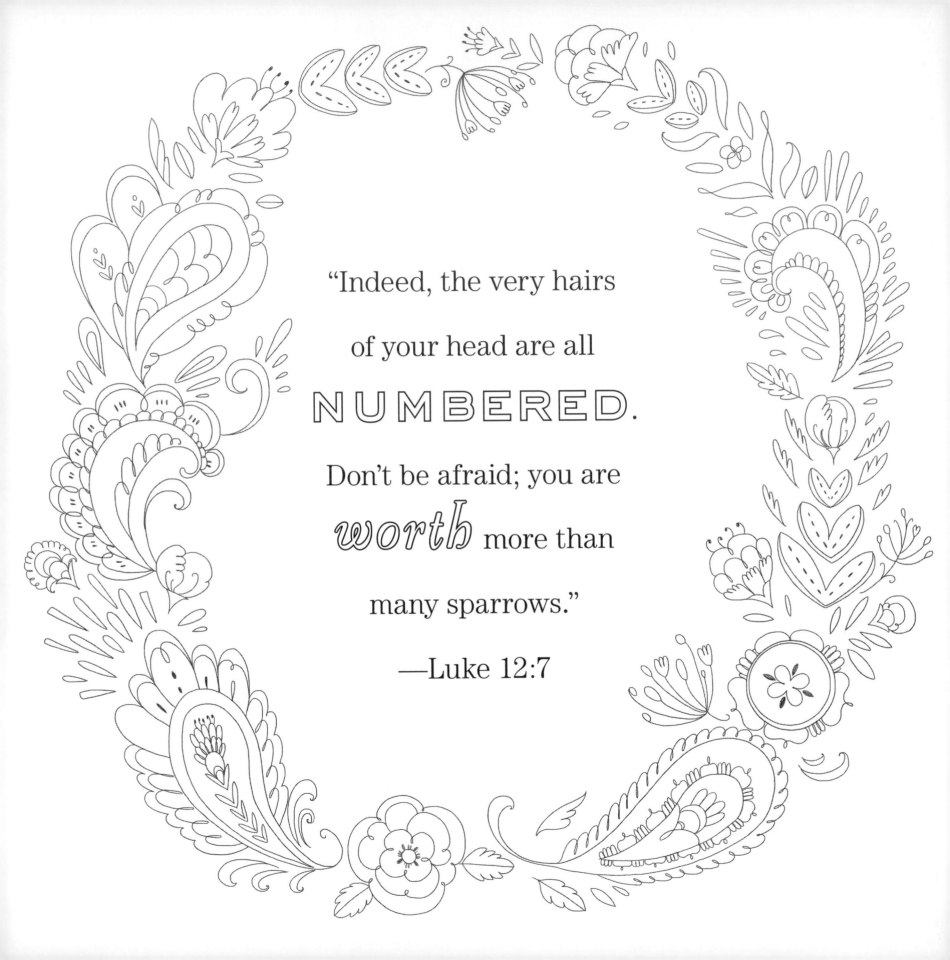

"Indeed, the very hairs

of your head are all

NUMBERED.

Don't be afraid; you are

worth more than

many sparrows."

—Luke 12:7

Marvel at the beauty of a life intertwined with my presence

When you walk through

a day with **childlike** delight,

savoring every *blessing*,

you proclaim your trust in Me,

your ever-present SHEPHERD.

Your inner calm—
YOUR
Peace
IN
my presence—
need not be
shaken
by what is going on
AROUND YOU.

Marvel at the *wonder* of being able to commune with the King of the universe—any time, any place. Never take this amazing privilege for granted! "I am the vine; you are the branches. He who ABIDES in Me, and I in him, bears much fruit; for without Me you can do nothing." —John 15:5 NKJV

Rather than
planning &
evaluating &
practice
& trusting
& thanking
Me continually.

Be WILLING

to go out on a limb with Me. If that

is where I am *leading* you,

it is the SAFEST place to be.

I will lie down & sleep in peace, for you alone, O Lord, make me dwell in safety.

Psalm 4:8

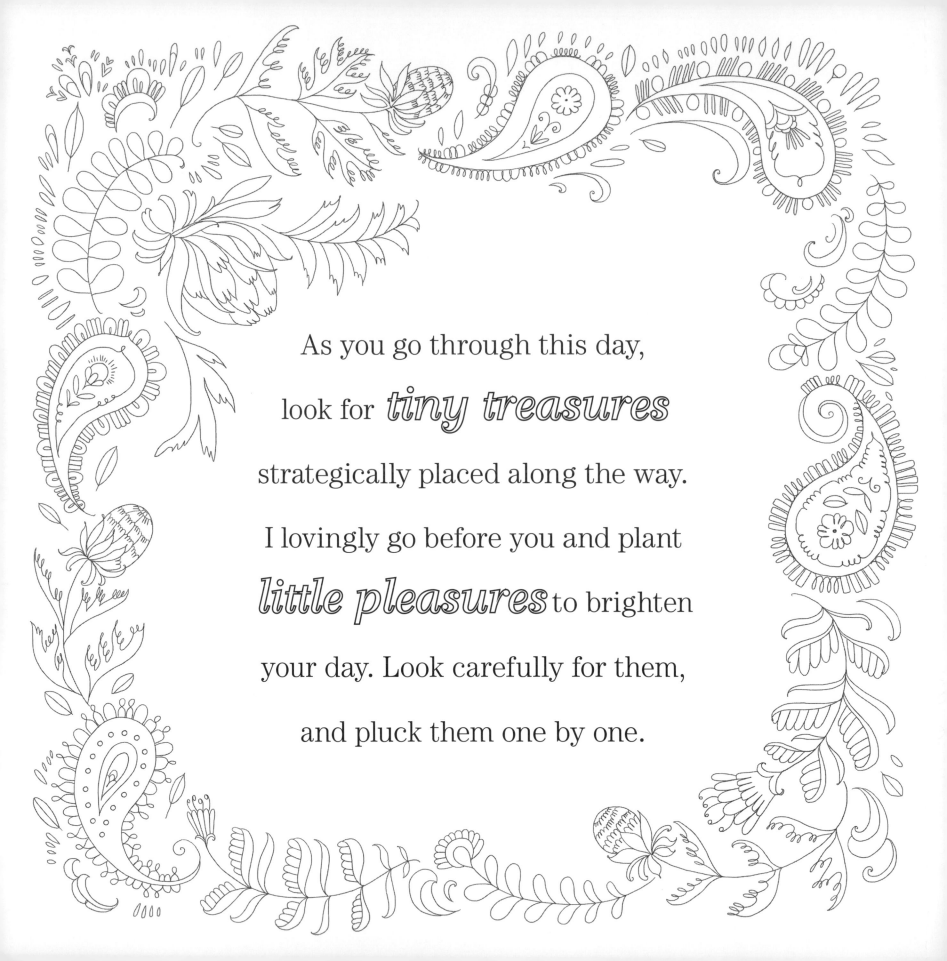

As you go through this day,

look for *tiny treasures*

strategically placed along the way.

I lovingly go before you and plant

little pleasures to brighten

your day. Look carefully for them,

and pluck them one by one.

But I am like an olive tree

flourishing

in the house of God; I trust

in God's unfailing LOVE for

ever and ever. —Psalm 52:8

Practice TRUSTING Me
during quiet days, when nothing
much seems to be happening.
Then when storms come,
your trust BALANCE will be
sufficient to see you through.

Practice Pages

Aa Bb Cc Dd Ee

Ff Gg Hh Ii Jj

Kk Ll Mm Nn Oo

Pp Qq Rr Ss Tt Uu

Vv Ww Xx Yy Zz